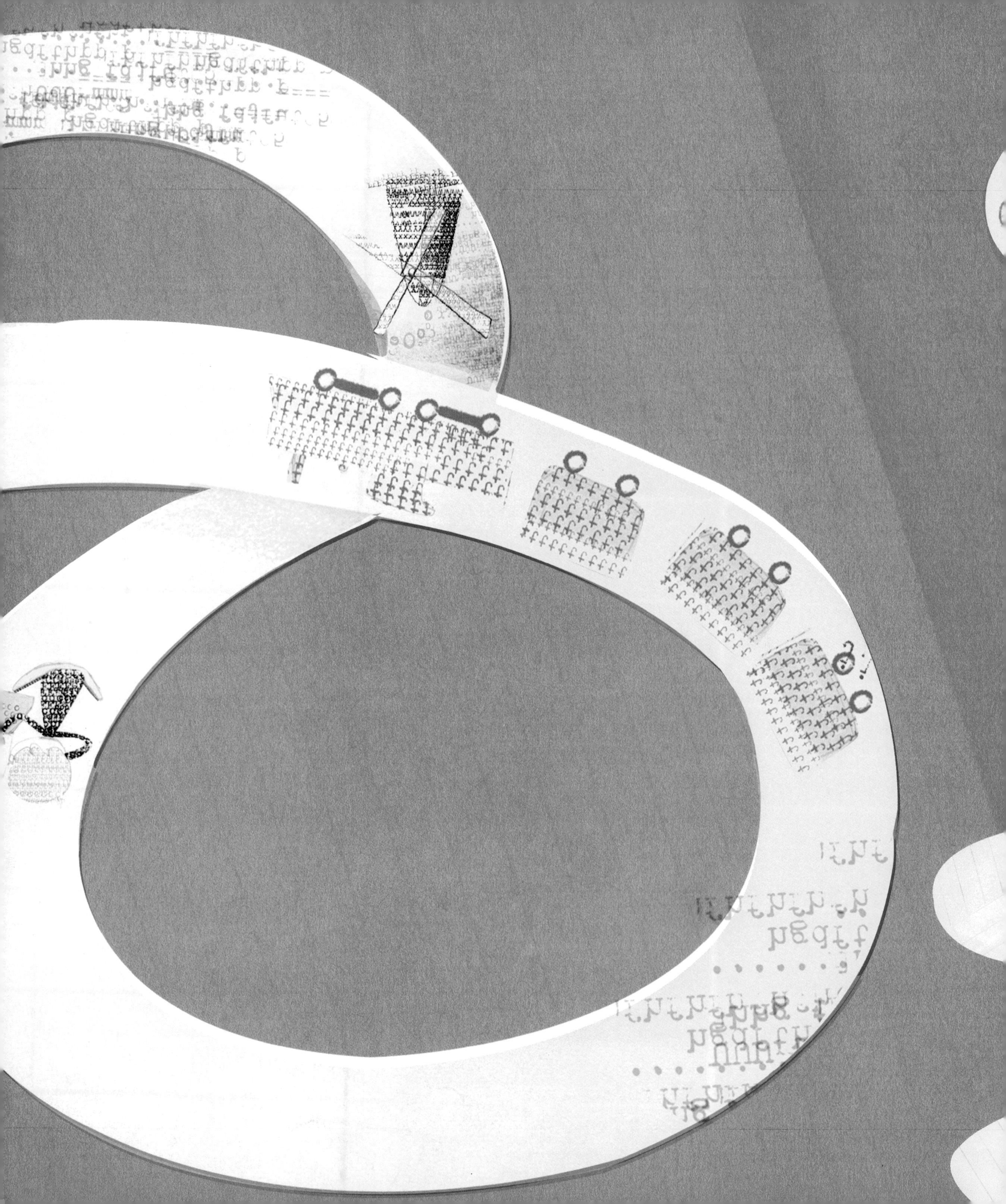

The Story Machine

Tom McLaughlin

BLOOMSBURY

LONDON NEW DELHI NEW YORK SYDNEY

Meet Elliott. Elliott was a boy
who loved to find things...

And, one day, he found a machine.

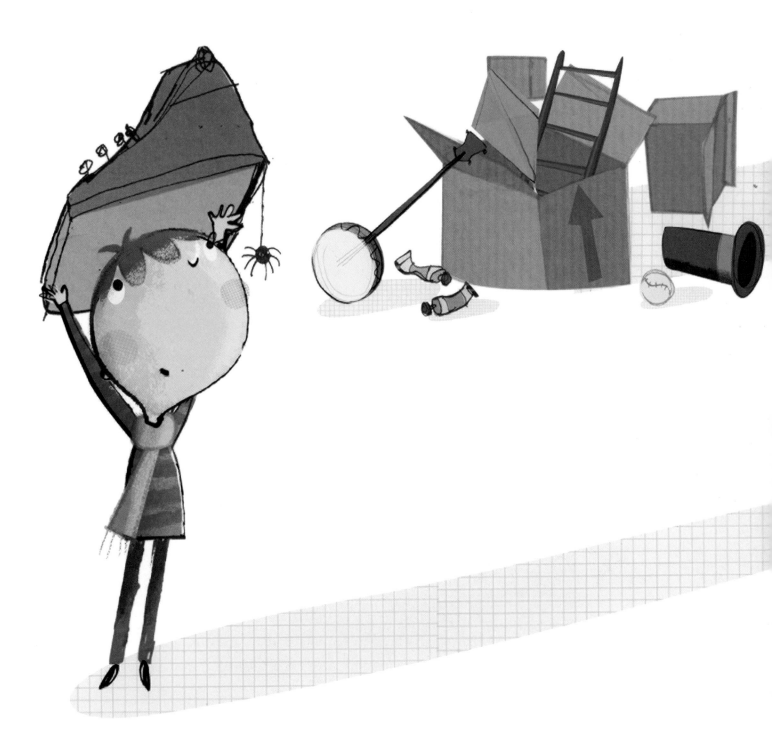

It didn't have an ON/OFF button
and it didn't even **bleep** or **buzz!**

Elliott was puzzled.

What did it do?

Then, quite by accident, he made it work.

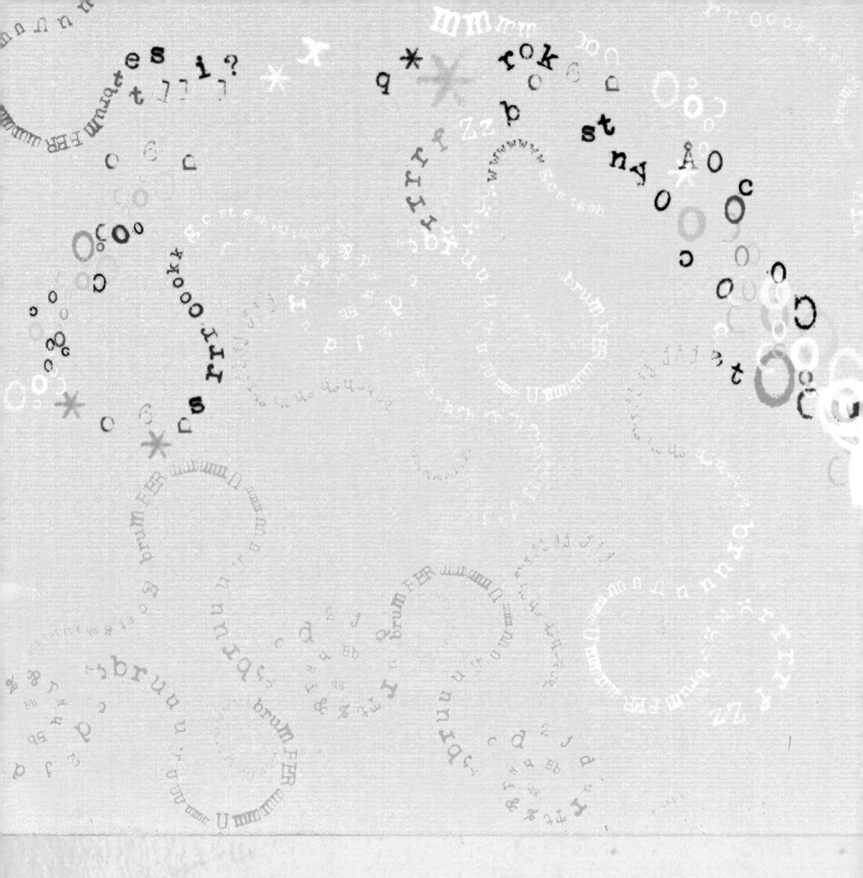

The machine made letters. And the letters made words. Perhaps it was a **story machine!**

Elliott, however, wasn't very good at letters.

He did his best, but he kept
getting them all jumbled up.

wonce
up
onn a
tyme

zzzz   sqweek   plop

Then Elliott noticed something
amongst the letters - a picture!

So Elliott began to make pictures...

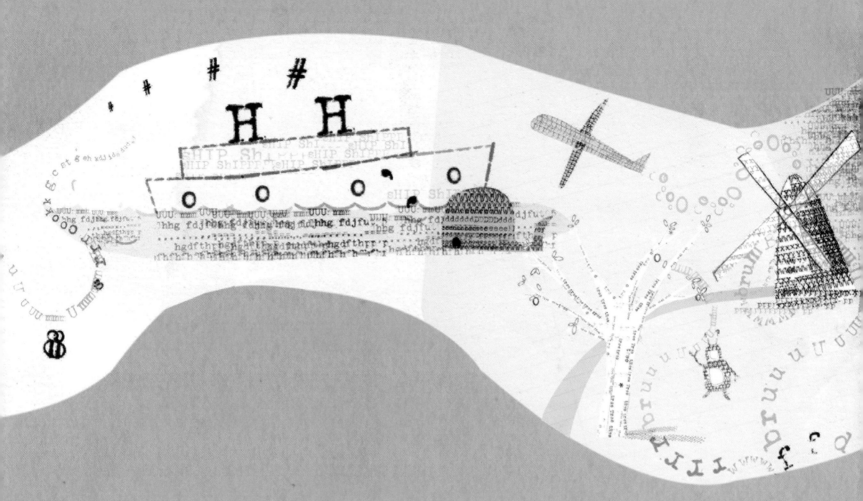

and once he started he just couldn't stop.

He made big pictures, small pictures, busy pictures and quiet pictures.

But the best thing about all his pictures was that they told a story.

Maybe it **was** a story machine after all!

But it didn't take long for things to go wrong.

Elliott had used the story machine
so much it had begun to malfunction.

No more machine!

That meant no more pictures
and no more stories.

Elliott was blue.

Until he found something else -
and that was when he realised
something very important...

It **wasn't** the machine that was making the stories...

...it was him and he was really rather good at it!

Elliott

For Mum x

With many thanks to Catherine Cartwright

Bloomsbury Publishing, London, New Delhi, New York and Sydney

First published in Great Britain in 2014 by Bloomsbury Publishing Plc
50 Bedford Square, London, WC1B 3DP

This paperback edition first published in 2015

A CIP catalogue record for this book is available from the British Library

ISBN 978 1 4088 3933 1 (HB)
ISBN 978 1 4088 3934 8 (PB)
ISBN 978 1 4088 3932 4 (eBook)

Printed in China by Leo Paper Products, Heshan, Guangdong

1 3 5 7 9 10 8 6 4 2

www.bloomsbury.com

All papers used by Bloomsbury Publishing are natural, recyclable products
made from wood grown in well-managed forests.
The manufacturing processes conform to the environmental regulations of the country of origin

BLOOMSBURY is a registered trademark of Bloomsbury Publishing Plc